THINK ABOUT

Having a
LEARNING
DISABILITY

Margaret and Peter Flynn

Smart Apple Media

First published in the UK in 1998 by

Belitha Press Limited
London House, Great Eastern Wharf,
Parkgate Road, London SW11 4NQ

Text and illustrations copyright © Belitha Press Limited 1998
Cover design by Kathy Petelinsek

Published in the United States by
Smart Apple Media
123 South Broad Street
Mankato, Minnesota 56001

Library of Congress Cataloging-in-Publication Data

Flynn, Margaret C.
Having a learning disability / Margaret and Peter Flynn.
p. cm. — (Think about)
Includes index.
Summary: Describes what it is like to have a learning disability and how different people
handle the challenges these difficulties present.
ISBN 1-887068-86-4
1. Learning disabled children—Education—Juvenile literature.   2. Learning disabilities—
Juvenile literature.   [1. Learning disabilities.]   I. Flynn, Peter, 1950–.   II. Title.
III. Series: Think about (Mankato, Minn.)

LC4704.F58   1999
371.9—dc21   98-34009

9   8   7   6   5   4   3

Photographs by: Anglia Press Agency, Collections (Anthea Sieveking), Paul Bryans, Cunnah
family, Down's Syndrome Association, Rachel Morton, Sara Hannant, Mary Evans Picture
Library, Margaret & Peter Flynn, Format Photographers, Joanne O'Brien, Maggie Murray,
Paula Solloway, Ulrike Preuss, Getty Images, David Woodfall, John Beatty, Lori Adamski
Peek, Peter Cade, Peter Correz, Ronald Grant Archive, Sally & Richard Greenhill, Robert
Harding Picture Library, The Lancaster Centre, Lancashire County Council, Martin Law,
The Lifetime Company, London Metropolitan Archive, McKean family, National Autistic
Society, Steve Hickey, Powerstock, Russell family, Scope, Scotsman Publications/Tomatis
Centre, Anya Souza & Paul Adeline, Stockmarket, Superstock, John Walmsley Photo Library

Words in **bold** are explained in the glossary on pages 30 and 31.

ABOUT THE AUTHORS

Margaret and Peter Flynn, who are sister and brother, cowrote this book. Peter, who has a learning disability, has written sections from his perspective that are found throughout the book.

Contents

What is a learning disability?

People with learning disabilities have lifelong difficulties in learning, understanding, and thinking clearly. Some people also have difficulties in seeing, walking, and taking care of themselves. There is no cure for learning disabilities, but people who have them can get help to reach goals and realize their dreams.

These children all have learning disabilities. About three percent of the people in the United States have a learning disability. They have different talents, qualities, strengths, and needs, just like everyone else.

What does it mean?

Peter: *To me a learning disability means someone who has learning problems and can't do things quickly and your ability to do things quickly is slower than you want. Sometimes you don't work as fast as others. I don't think people would want to have a learning disability because it could make them unhappy. Also people might pick on you.*

Judging by appearances

Many people who achieve fame and popularity, such as movie stars or pro athletes, are good-looking, strong, or fashionable. We often judge people by the way they look; but this doesn't tell us much about what someone is really like or how they feel. Some people with learning disabilities are treated badly by others who don't think about their feelings or personality.

Children who have learning disabilities have the same interests as most children. Jack, who has a learning disability, plays in a pool of balls with a friend.

The film *Forrest Gump* is about a man with a learning disability. In the past, there haven't been many heroes or heroines with learning disabilities in movies or books.

Things you should know

People's learning disabilities are not always obvious. A learning disability doesn't mean that a person can't learn at all; it just means that it often takes him more time and effort to learn. Many times, a person can't tell that someone has a learning disability just by looking at him.

Peter: *This is important. We have the same rights as everyone. Sometimes we need a bit of help.*

THINK ABOUT

Language

Think about names that you may have been called or that you have called someone else. Words such as "idiot" or "retard" are used to hurt people's feelings. Why do you think these names hurt? How would they make you feel?

Facts about learning disabilities

We don't always know why people have learning disabilities; often, no cause can be found. But we do know that babies are affected in various ways before, during, or just after birth that can result in damage to the **brain** or **spinal cord**.

The central nervous system

The part of the body that controls everything a person does is called the **central nervous system**. It is made up of the brain and spinal cord. The brain sends messages along the spinal cord and through the **nerves** to all parts of the body, telling them what to do. These parts send messages back to the brain. If parts of the brain or spinal cord are damaged, this system of nerves can't work as quickly or as well.

brain

spinal cord

nerves

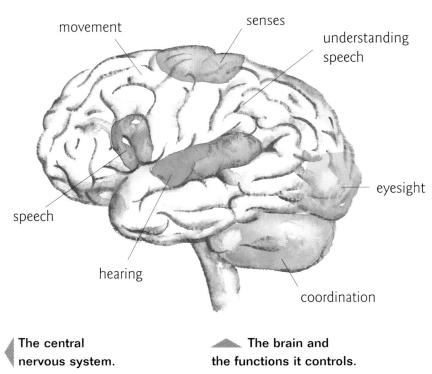

movement

senses

understanding speech

eyesight

speech

hearing

coordination

The central nervous system.

The brain and the functions it controls.

6

Different influences

Sometimes the parents of a baby have conditions that can be **inherited**. This means that the baby may have learning disabilities.

Babies sometimes have infections or illnesses before or just after they are born. Other times, babies don't get enough **oxygen** when they are born or don't weigh enough. All of these problems can lead to a learning disability in the child.

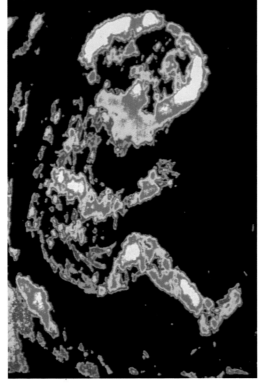

This photograph shows a baby growing inside its mother. At this stage, it is called a fetus. If the mother doesn't eat a good diet, or if she drinks a lot of alcohol, takes drugs, or has an infection, the baby could develop conditions that result in learning disabilities.

Environmental problems

The world around us can affect the development of unborn babies in ways that we don't fully understand. For example, chemical weapons used in wars can harm people for many **generations**.

Toxins are poisons that can harm plants, animals, or people when they are released into the **environment**.

THINK ABOUT

Finding out more

Our **genes** control our physical appearance. Genes are passed on from our parents, which is why some people look like their parents. Sometimes genes lead to people having learning disabilities. Try to learn more about genes.

Different learning disabilities

Sometimes people with learning disabilities have **physical** or **sensory** disabilities as well. Some people with learning disabilities may have cerebral palsy, Down **syndrome**, spina bifida, or autism.

Cerebral palsy

Cerebral palsy affects muscles, so people with the disease may have difficulty controlling their arm and leg movements. People with cerebral palsy might also have problems communicating clearly.

Down syndrome

People with Down syndrome have an extra **chromosome** in their body that gives them certain characteristics. For example, many people with the disability have eyes with a slight upward slant and fingers that are shorter than usual.

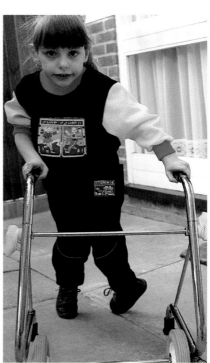

This girl has cerebral palsy. She uses a walker to help in moving around.

This girl with Down syndrome enjoys being with her friends.

This boy has spina bifida and uses a wheelchair to get around.

Spina bifida

Spina bifida is a disease in which part of a person's spinal cord and the nerves that control their muscles haven't developed normally. People with spina bifida often have trouble controlling the movement of their limbs, so they use wheelchairs to move around.

People often don't realize that a child has autism; they might think that the child just behaves badly. Autistic children need proper help and support.

Autism

Autism affects the way that people behave. Autistic children are often described as being in a world of their own, and they might not react to other people or loud noises. Sometimes they have trouble **communicating** with other people, and they might make strange noises instead of speaking. However, this behavior doesn't mean that they are not interested or not listening.

THINK ABOUT

Support

People who have learning disabilities need different kinds of help at different times in their lives. Even people with severe handicaps that limit their communication can make the most of their lives with the right support. What kinds of support do you need?

Looking back

Throughout history, people with learning disabilities have been feared, misunderstood, and pitied. As a result, people with learning disabilities were often rejected by their **communities**. Hospitals, **asylums**, and **institutions** were built to look after them, causing many people to be separated from their families.

Living away from home

In the past, many children with learning disabilities were sent to live in institutions. Their parents believed that they would receive better care in these places. But in many of these homes, people did not get proper health care. Children were not educated, and some were treated cruelly. It was difficult for families to visit and keep in touch.

There were separate asylums for men and women. Girls and boys were separated too—even brothers and sisters. This drawing shows a Paris asylum for women in 1871.

Peter: *I think this is terrible. Asylums might have started off with good intentions but they all went wrong. I went round an institution once. There were 50 beds in one dormitory. Everyone looked the same. They even had the same clothes on. I didn't want to live there and I felt it was terrible for those who had to.*

This cartoon from 1880 shows a boy being punished for not learning his lessons. Years ago, many children who found their school work difficult were not given extra help or support.

Controlling lives

In the past, doctors have tried to prevent disabled children from being born; they have also stopped some disabled people from having children of their own. These types of attempts to control people's lives are very upsetting to many people with disabilities.

Labeling people

People with learning disabilities have been labeled as subnormal, mentally retarded, mentally defective, and mentally handicapped. Such labels hurt people by making them feel less than human.

Peter: *These are stupid names. They make me feel sad because there's no need for them. All these labels are hurtful. . . .*

This girl is taking an intelligence test in 1907. These tests were used to figure out a person's "mental age." Such tests were usually meaningless and insulting.

THINK ABOUT

Being sent away

Imagine being taken away from your family and growing up without them. How would your parents, brothers, or sisters feel? Often, parents didn't want their disabled child to be sent away, but they weren't given any other choice. How are things different today?

At home

Children belong in families. Most babies and children with learning disabilities grow up with their parents, brothers, and sisters. Their family and friends quickly learn that although they may need a helping hand to do some things, they have their own special gifts and abilities, just like all children.

Part of the family

Children with learning disabilities can live with their family if they receive the kind of help they need. Special equipment such as wheelchair **ramps** can be built onto houses for disabled children. Some families want helpers who will make sure that their child has the chance to go out and meet other children. Some parents want **advocates** who will help them get the best services for their disabled child.

◀ There are many families that have disabled children with special needs. Everyone in a family needs love and affection. Family members should help and support each other.

Having a happy home

In the past, many children with learning disabilities lived in special homes because their parents could not take care of them without extra help. Other families weren't allowed to **adopt** them, so the children grew up without a family. Today, babies and children with learning disabilities can be adopted.

Peter: *Babies are best with families who will love them and cuddle them and show them what a loving family life is about.*

Peter grew up with his family. This is him as a boy with Margaret (left) and their sisters.

THINK ABOUT

Families

If you had a brother or a sister with a learning disability, what kind of help do you think your family would need? Families of children with learning disabilities need different kinds of support. They might need someone to help out at home, or they might need special transportation to help their child get around. The help they need will change as the child grows older.

Having fun

Danny has a learning disability. This is what his older sister Lianne says about him:

*"My brother Danny has learning disabilities. It happened after his **vaccine**. Danny is very special to me. It's hard for him to talk and understand. Danny is six years old. His talking is getting . . . better now. His problem is hard to understand to some people. Danny can read some words and stories. At night, me and Danny read a book together. We read all his favorite stories. Danny is a boy who is like you and you are just like him. When I am older I will care about him still."*

13

At school

Many children with learning disabilities take **special education** classes. A lot of young children with learning disabilities go to **integrated day care centers**, and many families want their children to go to ordinary schools as well.

▼ Disabled and non-disabled children can learn and have fun together.

Special education

In the past, children who had learning disabilities did not go to school. Although this has changed, many families today do not like special education because their children don't learn and play with non-disabled children. Parents don't want to see their children miss out on these important experiences.

Ordinary schools

There are many advantages to sending all children to local schools. Disabled and non-disabled children can learn a lot from each other and become good friends. Children with learning disabilities have the same interests at school as most other children.

Peter: *[Cooking] was the best at school because we made different things to eat which I enjoyed very much because we tasted them afterwards. I liked the [cooking] teacher very much. She was a very understanding teacher and she used to take us places. Even when I was little I liked going places.*

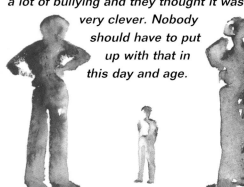

▲ These children are learning using big, bright pictures and lots of help from the teacher.

Making the change

If all children are to be sent to their local school, a lot of work will be needed to change the school system. Teachers and principals have to be enthusiastic about making changes in their school. They need to find ways of teaching that include attention to all children.

Being bullied

Learning-disabled children and their families often worry about bullying at school.

Peter: *My school days were very bad. One teacher scared me very much. When we were in the dining room it was so noisy. I didn't like the playground. There was a lot of bullying and they thought it was very clever. Nobody should have to put up with that in this day and age.*

▼ These learning-disabled children go to their local elementary school. Here they are working in art class.

Peter: *The teacher should make all the lessons interesting for everybody so that everyone can join in. It helps to have an extra teacher in class who works with small groups of people. This helps everyone in the small groups. Sometimes older children can help as well by listening to them read or something like that.*

15

Thoughts and feelings

No one likes to be ignored, teased, or bullied. People with learning disabilities can get hurt or angry about the way they are treated by others. Everyone shows feelings in different ways, but some feelings are hard to share.

Expressing yourself
One group of people with learning disabilities has thought hard about the hurt, anger, and sadness caused by **discrimination**. They paint, write poetry, and perform plays to show that people with learning disabilities have the same kinds of thoughts and feelings as everyone else. Their work is called Heartstone.

▲ This is the Heartstone group. They use writing, art, and drama to express their thoughts and feelings.

Their plays and artwork show how communities are made up of many different kinds of people. Everyone has times when they need help and times when they can help others. The group says:

"We take the display to schools and local businesses to show people that we are not mad or looneys. We are actual people with feelings and also deserve a purpose in life."

Dealing with negative feelings

Paul has a learning disability. What does this mean to him, and how does it make him feel?

"For me it is not being able to understand what is going on, feeling that I can't quite put things together, always lagging behind and being left out because people do not know how to take my seemingly bad-tempered remarks."

"If someone asks me a question, I can give a clear answer, but it sometimes takes me such a long time that they usually lose interest half-way through what I have to say. Sometimes people will spoon-feed me or, what is worse, show badly hidden impatience with me. Both these reactions leave me feeling stupid and worthless. Putting a lid on the negative feelings which come up is difficult. The pressure can become so great that I just explode or have a panic attack, hurting everyone around me."

This is Paul and Anya. You can read about Anya on page 25.

Peter: *Paul is not stupid. He makes us all think.*

We all feel better about ourselves if we are given a chance to use and develop our skills. This teenager is taking a computer course at her college.

THINK ABOUT

Speaking out

Peter: *Children with learning disabilities do get worried and sometimes panic if they can't keep up with other children.*

Have you ever felt worried when you couldn't do difficult math or read complicated words? Have other people ever made you feel sad, confused, or angry?
Talking to someone about our feelings can help us to understand our problems and to begin to sort them out.

Communication

Everyone needs to be able to communicate. It is the way we send and receive messages or let others know what we are thinking or feeling. Some people with learning disabilities do not talk, read, or write. Their family and friends need to find different ways to communicate with them.

These children at day care are learning to copy the movements their teacher makes.

Ways of learning

If people don't read or write, there are other ways that they can share what they are thinking or feeling. They might use signs, **gestures**, or sounds that people who know them well can understand. Some children who don't speak very clearly can use a computerized **speech synthesizer**.

Teachers of children with learning disabilities do not use complicated words. They use pictures to show what words mean, and they may teach some children signs to help them communicate more easily. Some people with learning disabilities prefer to listen to words on tape instead of trying to read them.

Learning to smile

Alexander has a learning disability, but his mom is proud of his communication skills.

"My name is Eileen and I have two children, Alexander and Charlotte. They are very special. Alexander is very handsome with beautiful blue eyes and a lovely smile. He also has a learning disability, does not walk or talk, and has no sight."

The TV program *Sesame Street* helps disabled and non-disabled children learn to spell and count.

Alexander and his sister Charlotte.

"This means he needs lots more help than his sister, who has no disabilities, but who also has a lovely smile. Alexander loves you to touch and hold his hands. His greatest joy is [soccer]. Although it took Alexander five years to learn to smile, he often does now, especially when we all shout 'goal!' "

Body language

There are many ways to communicate. People don't have to speak to communicate. We smile, frown, and use our hands to wave or point. We can see how other people are feeling by their facial expressions or gestures. Some people with learning disabilities don't show their feelings, but there are still ways of communicating with them.

THINK ABOUT

Joining in

Can you imagine going through a day without speaking? How would you let other people know what you wanted or how you were feeling? How would you join in activities with your friends? Try to think of signs that you could use to communicate simple things. Think about how you would ask a friend to play a game with you, or how you could tell them that you were feeling tired or sick. Try out these signs with your friends.

Fun and games

Children with learning disabilities have the same kinds of hobbies and interests as other kids. They often like watching TV, drawing, or playing sports with other children. Other learning-disabled children may take dancing classes or music lessons. Children with learning disabilities can join the same clubs as all children their age.

Hobbies

Everyone should have a chance to do the things they like. But sometimes things can prevent children with learning disabilities from joining in sports and other activities. Some children use wheelchairs, but many buildings are not **adapted** for wheelchair users. Other children with learning disabilities don't join clubs or activities because they don't have friends to go along with them.

▲ Many people enjoy swimming. It is a great activity for having fun and making friends.

Toys

All babies and children need to play and have toys that help them develop their senses and learn about the world around them. Children with learning disabilities don't always play on their own; they often need help from their family. Children who can't control their movements very well sometimes push toys away without meaning to. Today there are specially made toys that can be attached to a table.

Having fun

What do you like to do in your spare time?

Peter: *I remember playing hide and seek when I was little. I didn't like jigsaw puzzles but neither did my sisters. None of us can do them! I didn't like [soccer]. I used to miss the ball. I used to like party games . . . and playing on the swings in the park.*

Playing with friends

Peter: *In the past, babies and children with learning disabilities had to go to special nurseries. I think this was a bad idea because they weren't allowed to mix with other children. Playing with other children is a good way for young children to learn about the world and to discover new things.*

▼ Many people enjoy playing musical instruments. This learning-disabled girl loves to make music.

◢ These play areas are fun for all children—with or without disabilities. There are lots of soft, colorful toys to play with.

Going to work

Most young people have some idea of what they would like to do for a living when they grow up. But some people aren't allowed to fulfill these dreams. Many people with learning disabilities are not given the chance to work and earn money.

Peter: *When I was [in special education] they didn't ask me what I wanted to do. You just went to [a training center].They didn't talk to us about careers. Looking back, it was a bad decision because no one asked me and I couldn't understand why they were doing it. I hope that this doesn't happen to special education [graduates] now.*

▷ This man, who has a learning disability, found his job as a cook through a supported employment service.

Finding a job

Most adults with severe learning disabilities don't have jobs, even though they would like to work. Many of them go to day care centers, where they often feel like they are wasting their time. They often don't have many chances to meet non-disabled people.

Today there is a service called supported employment. It helps people with learning disabilities to think about the sort of job they would like and to train for the job. Supported employment lets people have real jobs, real wages, and the chance to make friends at work.

These people have decided to take courses at college.

Going to college

Some people with learning disabilities choose to go to college and learn new skills.

Peter: *I used to go to a day center. It was awful. All you did all day was put screws in boxes and fold paper hats. It was degrading. Since I have left I have done lots of interesting things which I have found more meaningful, like* **volunteer work** *and going to college. At college I do basic computing which is fulfilling. People in my room need a little bit of help, which I need myself.*

Learning and working

Simon is a learning-disabled man who enjoys working and going to college.

"I go to college two days a week. I do painting and design. I like painting best. Then I go to . . . a center where we grow flowers. We make dried flowers and take them to hotels. I like helping mend machinery, mowers, and things like that. We have lots of friends [there]. . . . Sometimes Len [the instructor] takes us out on jobs. We do gardens. There are a lot of gardens down here. People like flowers."

This is Simon with his dog Lucy. Simon's goals are to have a full-time job and to become an artist.

 **THINK ABOUT**

Ordinary lives

People with learning disabilities would like to lead ordinary lives and do all the things that most people take for granted, such as having a job, earning money, deciding where to live, and visiting new places. It is very important to give people with learning disabilities the support they need to do these things.

Making changes

The world we live in can be changed for the better. There are new services that are improving many people's lives. These services are helping more and more children with learning disabilities to go to ordinary schools, reach goals, and form lifelong friendships.

Speaking out

Speaking for ourselves is very important. Most of us learn how to do this, but some people will always need help. People First is the name of an organization that brings together people with learning disabilities and helps them to make positive changes in their lives.

The goal of People First is to teach people with learning disabilities to speak up for themselves and to use their rights. The organization gives talks to groups and speaks at conferences.

All people should be able to lead the life they choose. This couple wanted to be together and decided to get married.

Taking control

Anya has Down syndrome, but it hasn't stopped her from having a full, busy, and interesting life.

"My father is a painter and my mother was an actress. I work in stained glass. I make mirrors and candle holders. I am also an actress. Sometimes I speak at conferences and make videos for TV. Often I speak up for the rights of people with Down syndrome. I do not like the way I have been treated at school. I was bullied. Now that I am an adult things seem to be a lot better. When people call me a person with learning difficulties, I really don't understand what they mean. I have a LIFE!"

▲ **Anya speaking at a conference. She works hard and enjoys seeing her friends and boyfriend.**

◀ **This man lives in his own house and gets help with housework such as ironing clothes.**

Homes of our own

Most people would like to have their own home when they are older. Supported living lets adults with learning disabilities live in their own homes with the extra help and support that they need.

(**THINK** **ABOUT**)

Campaigning

New services are often created because a lot of people have campaigned for them. Many parents and families of children with learning disabilities work to improve schools.

Peter: *This reminds me of my mom. She was the secretary of a local parent's group. It makes me proud to think that she was doing a lot of work for me and lots of other people. I think she'd be very pleased if she was here to see me writing a book.*

Being a success

Everyone wants to be a success at something, but people with learning disabilities often have to work extra hard to persuade others to give them a chance. But with the right help and encouragement, disabled people can achieve a lot, even if their accomplishments —such as learning to read or taking part in a conversation—seem very ordinary to most people.

Standing up for yourself

Jackie knows how important it is to be a part of the community. She says:

"When I was at school, they said I had a a moderate learning disability, but I really don't know what that is or what it means. When I was growing up, the main thing I realized in my life is that children should have a voice. We are people. We should have rights and choices. Sometimes people think we can't contribute to society by looking at our disabilities and not our capabilities. Especially in school, children should be aware that everyone should be heard, especially disabled children. A lot of children have special gifts— we shouldn't lose that."

▶ **This is Jackie. Going to college helped her realize that people need rights. She worries that many people with learning disabilities are not given the help and support they need to make the most of their lives.**

Learning together

Most people with learning disabilities achieve more than others ever expected them to. When Luke was born, his parents were told that he would never walk or talk. But with lots of help from his family and doctor, Luke started to communicate and learned to walk.

Luke surpassed most people's expectations by learning to talk, smile, and hug his parents.

The way forward

Peter: *Disabled people have got so much to offer. It would be better if people stopped looking at everything we can't do and looked at what we can do.*

Most people wouldn't think that disabled people could climb a mountain. But with the right help and support, people with disabilities can do almost anything.

THINK ABOUT

Talent

What are your talents? Maybe you're a fast runner, a good listener, or a computer whiz. Maybe you can make people laugh. Everyone is good at something.

Looking to the future

Life for people with learning disabilities is better now than it used to be, but there is still a long way to go. For many people with learning disabilities, ordinary things to most people—such as living on their own when they grow up and making decisions about their future—are still a dream.

What needs to be done?

There are still too many adults and children with learning disabilities who go unnoticed because they are separated from the rest of the community, causing them to miss out on many opportunities and experiences. Parents of children with learning disabilities would like to see a more integrated society. As more people with learning disabilities speak out and become leaders, they will help others to realize that all people have rights and abilities.

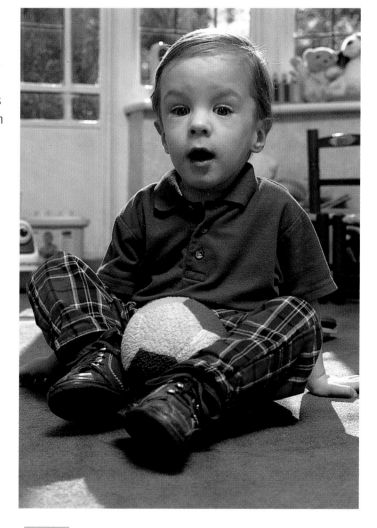

No one can predict what this boy will achieve in the future. He has his own strengths, talents, and ideas, just like all children.

Human rights

If people with learning disabilities are to have meaningful and fulfilling lives, they will need to be able to take advantage of their human rights. Everyone should know and use their rights and make sure that others are able to do the same.

Peter: *It's our lives and we should make decisions or be helped to by people who love us.*

In the future, this student may encourage other people with learning disabilities to speak for themselves and defend their rights.

Everyone likes to have friends to share a joke or a laugh.

The last word

Peter: *I understand my own learning disability because I have learned to live with it. I sing and I enjoy music. I've got lots of records and tapes and I like listening to Irish music. I go out on my own and I travel on my own. I do volunteer work. I do errands for people, go shopping, and make cups of tea for visitors. I need help sometimes in my [apartment]. There are people who can't do things I can do. You need people to believe in you.*

THINK ABOUT

Making friends

Peter: *You should treat children with learning disabilities as normal and befriend them. Look out for them and make sure they're not pushed around. Say hello to them when they get to school, play with them in the school yard, and sit with them at dinner time. Get to know children with learning disabilities so that everyone's life is as enjoyable as possible.*

Glossary

adapted   Changed or improved. If a building is adapted for people who use wheelchairs, it might have a ramp outside.

adopt   To look after a child whose parents have died or are not able to take care of him. The adoptive parents bring up the child as their own.

asylum   see institution

brain   A very complicated and important part of the body that lets us think and controls all the body's activities, such as breathing and pumping blood throughout the body. Different parts of the brain control different areas of the body. (See diagram on page 6.)

central nervous system
The brain and the spinal cord. The nervous system controls everything the body does by sending and receiving messages along nerves that run to all parts of the body.

chromosome   A tiny part of a cell in the body. Usually each cell contains 46 chromosomes, but some people have cells that contain 47 chromosomes instead. This difference causes Down syndrome.

advocate   Someone who speaks for a person or a cause. Advocates for disabled people tell them what their rights are and help them to live the kinds of lives they want.

communicate   To pass thoughts or feelings from one person to another. There are many ways of communicating, such as speaking, writing, and making gestures and signals.

community   The people who live in a certain area or who share the same experiences. A community can be small, such as the people along a street, or large, such as everyone in a town or city.

day care centers   Places where many children and adults with learning disabilities spend their days. Many people

do not like this because they do not learn new skills or do things that they are interested in.

discrimination   Treating people unfairly because of their differences. These differences may be in skin color, age, or beliefs. People with learning disabilities may experience discrimination.

environmental   Having to do with the world around us— our homes, communities, and all of the factors and conditions that influence our lives.

generation   A stage in the history of a family. Children's parents are one generation, and the children are the next generation.

genes   Parts of the cells in a body that determine if a person is tall or short, or has dark or light skin. Parents pass their genes on to their children.

gesture   A movement of the hands, head, or body to communicate something.

inherited Something that is passed down to a child by her parents. Eye color, height, and other physical features in the parents' genes can all be inherited by the child.

institution A place that provides a specific kind of care or treatment for people. In the past, there were many institutions and asylums for people with learning disabilities. But most people with learning disabilities today live with their families.

integrated Made up of many different kinds of people. An integrated school includes all local children, both with and without disabilities.

nerve A tiny, thin connection that carries messages from the brain to all parts of the body.

oxygen A colorless gas in the air that we need to breathe to live.

physical Having to do with the body or its motion.

ramp A sloping floor or path used in place of—or in addition to—steps.

sensory Having to do with one or more of the senses.

special education Education that is just for some children—for example, children who are blind, deaf, or have learning disabilities. Special education classes give disabled children extra help and care.

speech synthesizer Computerized equipment that allows people to speak by typing or touching keys on a keyboard. A computer-generated voice speaks the words.

spinal cord Part of the body's central nervous system. Messages are passed from the brain along the spinal cord and to the nerves, which carry the messages to different parts of the body.

syndrome A set of signs and symptoms that are part of a certain condition.

vaccine A liquid that is injected or swallowed to protect against a disease. Drugs used in certain vaccines have caused learning disabilities in some babies.

volunteer work Work that someone chooses to do in their spare time for no pay.

Useful addresses

For more information about learning disabilities, contact these organizations or visit their web sites.

American Association on Mental Retardation
444 North Capitol Street NW, Suite 846
Washington, DC 20001
http://www.aamr.org/

BrightEye Technology
(technology for the learning-disabled)
2 Westwood Place
Asheville, NC 28806
http://www.brighteye.com

Independence Center
3640 South Sepulveda Blvd., Suite 102
Los Angeles, CA 90034
http://www.independencecenter.com/

Integra Foundation
25 Imperial Street
Toronto, ON M5P 1B9
http://www.iSTAR.ca/~integra/

Learning Disabilities Association
4156 Library Road
Pittsburgh, PA 15234
http://www.ldanatl.org/

Learning Disabilities Association of Canada
323 Chapel Street
Ottawa, ON K1N 7Z2
http://edu-ss10.educ.queensu.ca/~lda

National Academy for Child Development
The Weber Center
2380 Washington Blvd., 2nd Floor
Ogden, UT 84401
http://www.nacd.org/index.html

National Center for Learning Disabilities
381 Park Ave. South, Suite 1401
New York, NY 10016
http://www.ncld.org/

Index